P9-DXS-593

MAR - 2010   LI

WARNING!

Scaredy Squirrel insists that everyone check under their beds before reading this book.

To Joe, who dreams about getting a little more sleep

Text and illustrations © 2009 Mélanie Watt

All rights reserved. No part of this publication may be
reproduced, stored in a retrieval system or transmitted,
in any form or by any means, without the prior written
permission of Kids Can Press Ltd. or, in case of photocopying
or other reprographic copying, a license from The Canadian Copyright
Licensing Agency (Access Copyright). For an Access Copyright license,
visit www.accesscopyright.ca or call toll free to 1-800-893-5777.

Kids Can Press acknowledges the financial support of the Government of Ontario, through the Ontario
Media Development Corporation's Ontario Book Initiative; the Ontario Arts Council; the Canada
Council for the Arts; and the Government of Canada, through the BPIDP, for our publishing activity.

Published in Canada by
Kids Can Press Ltd.
29 Birch Avenue
Toronto, ON M4V 1E2

Published in the U.S. by
Kids Can Press Ltd.
2250 Military Road
Tonawanda, NY 14150

www.kidscanpress.com

The artwork in this book was rendered digitally in Photoshop.
The text is set in Potato Cut.

Edited by Tara Walker
Designed by Mélanie Watt and Karen Powers
Printed and bound in China

This book is smyth sewn casebound.

CM 09 0 9 8 7 6 5 4 3 2

LIBRARY AND ARCHIVES CANADA CATALOGUING IN PUBLICATION

Watt, Mélanie, 1975–
    Scaredy Squirrel at night / written and illustrated by Mélanie Watt.

ISBN 978-1-55453-288-9

1. Title.

PS8645.A88S2826 2009   jC813'.6   C2008-904793-1

Kids Can Press is a Corus™ Entertainment company

Scaredy Squirrel

at night

by Mélanie Watt

KIDS CAN PRESS

Scaredy Squirrel never sleeps.
He'd rather stay awake than risk having
a bad dream in the middle of the night.

A few creatures Scaredy Squirrel is afraid could appear in a bad dream:

dragons

fairies

ghosts

unicorns

vampire bats

polka-dot monsters

So he's very determined to stay awake
by keeping busy all through the night.

SCAREDY'S NIGHTTIME "TO DO" LIST

1. **Count stars**
(should keep you occupied for a while)

2. **Play cymbals**
(loud, annoying noise is sure to keep you wide awake)

3. **Take up scrapbooking**
(keeps you well-organized and productive)

So night
after night ...

after
night ...

after
night ...

Scaredy
avoids
sleeping.

BUT ...

SIDE EFFECTS OF SLEEPLESS NIGHTS MAY INCLUDE:

energy loss

forgetfulness

drowsiness

moodiness

poor reflexes

hallucinations

confusion ...

...and exhaustion!

That's when Scaredy Squirrel
comes face-to-face with
something very alarming ...

HOROSCOPES

FIND OUT WHAT THE STARS PREDICT FOR YOU!

 Aries (March 21–April 19)
You can climb mountains!

 Libra (Sept. 23– Oct. 22)
Get ready. At midnight all your dreams will come true!

 Taurus (April 20–May 20)
Take the bull by the horns!

Scorpio (Oct. 23–Nov. 21)
Look out or you'll be stung!

 Gemini (May 21–June 21)
Two heads are always better than one!

 Sagittarius (Nov. 22–Dec. 21)
Aim for your goals!

 Cancer (June 22–July 22)
Claw your way to success!

 Capricorn (Dec. 22–Jan. 19)
You're halfway there!

 Leo (July 23–Aug. 22)
You're the king of the jungle!

 Aquarius (Jan. 20–Feb. 18)
Go with the flow!

 Virgo (Aug. 23–Sept. 22)
Spread your wings and fly!

 Pisces (Feb. 19–March 20)
There are plenty of fish in the sea!

A few things Scaredy Squirrel needs to face his bad dreams:

spotlight

cupcakes

banana peels

fire extinguisher

safety cones

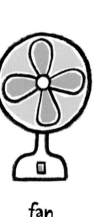

fan

teddy bear (decoy)

sign

pillow and blanket

molasses

BAD DREAM ACTION PLAN

Dragons are a huge fire hazard so keep extinguisher in tree!

Not a fan of ghosts? Start the breeze and they'll be blown away!

Molasses will slow down a unicorn in a sticky situation.

Place sign upside down so bats can read it.

Fairies have a sweet tooth — distract them with cupcakes!

Polka-dot monsters can't spot banana peels. Watch them slip and slide!

I am here.

Creatures think I am sleeping here.

 IMPORTANT: These creatures avoid light. Hide behind spotlight, switch it on at midnight and creatures will disappear! Remember, if all else fails, **PLAY DEAD** until sunrise.

So Scaredy Squirrel gets into position.
As he counts down to midnight, his bad
dreams seem to come true, one by one.

But when he turns on the spotlight ...

Hungry intruders appear!

This was NOT part of the Plan!

PLEASE CLEAN UP!

He slips and slides on a banana peel ...

He lands on the pillow ...

AND ...

PLAYS DEAD ...

and falls asleep!

1 hour later

2 hours later

8 hours later, Scaredy Squirrel finally wakes up.

BENEFITS OF A GOOD NIGHT'S SLEEP MAY INCLUDE:

energy gain

sharper memory

good health

happiness

better reflexes

peacefulness

cleverness ...

Scaredy Squirrel forgets all about his bad dreams. He realizes they were just in his imagination and nothing horrible happened in the night.

A good sleep has inspired him to get rid of a few things and replace his horoscope with something much more trustworthy ...